Have You Seen My MONSTER?

STEVE LIGHT

WALKER BOOKS
AND SUBSIDIARIES
LONDON · BOSTON · SYDNEY · AUCKLAND

Have you seen my monster?

No? Maybe he's already at the fair.

rectangle

octagon

He loves the carousel...

Did he go to judge the pies?

He loves the fun house …

and the bearded lady.

If he went to the egg display, I hope he's careful!

Maybe he went to see the livestock. I hope he doesn't scare the animals

square

Can you see my monster?

Has my monster been on this ride?

trapezium

MONSTER TRUCK CRASH!

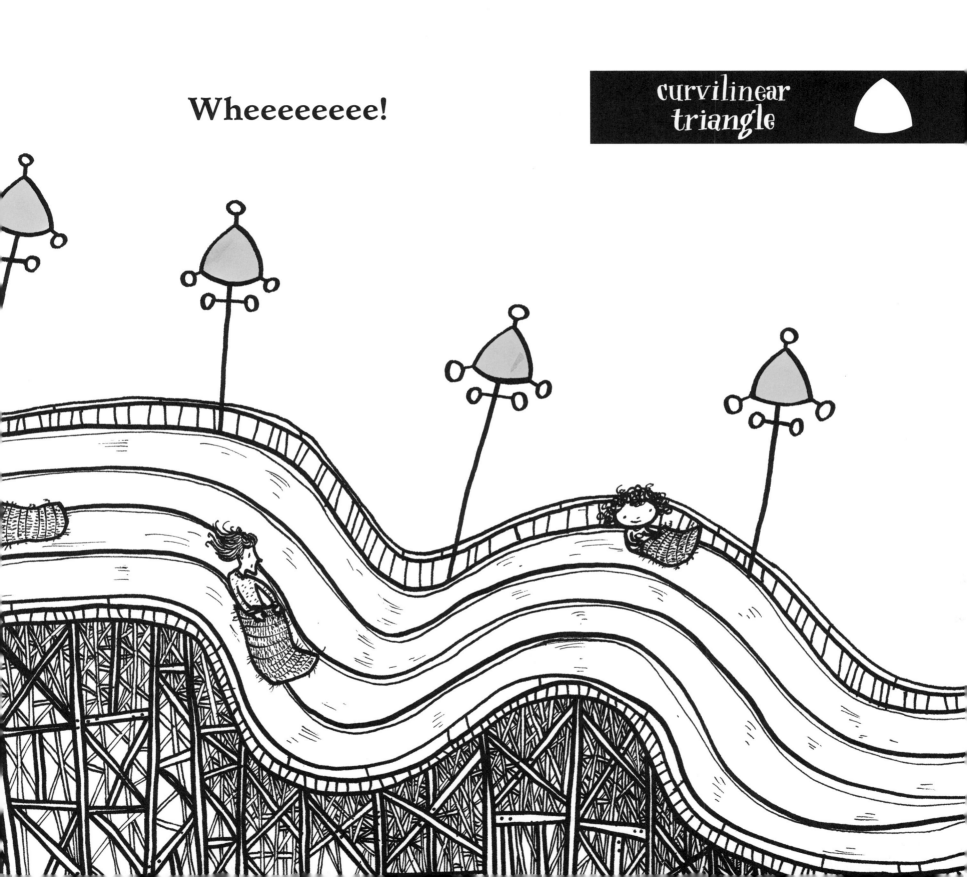

Wheeeeeeee!

curvilinear triangle

My monster may have needed a snack.

Maybe he –
bump,
bump,
bump –
came here.

heptagon

Perhaps I can see him from up here!

He's very good at crafts ...
maybe he won a prize!

He loves music!

pentagon

Where could he be?

Maybe up high ...

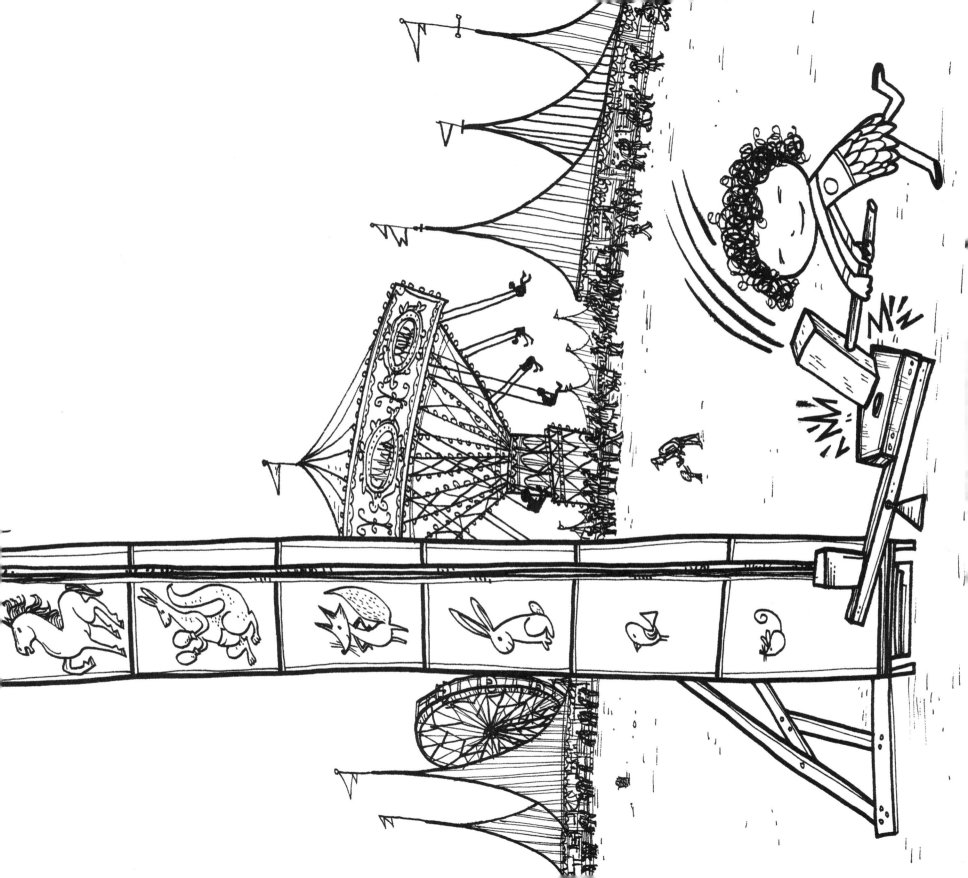

or just hanging out!

Oh, there he is!

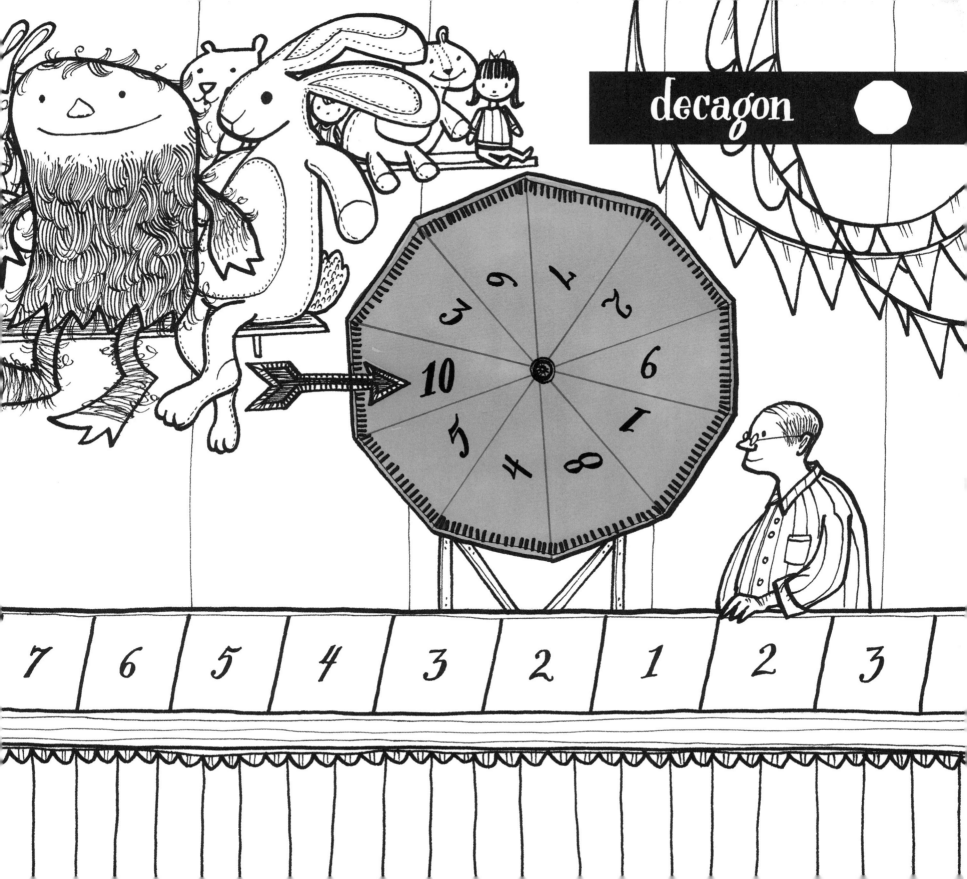

decagon

Time to take my monster home.

crescent

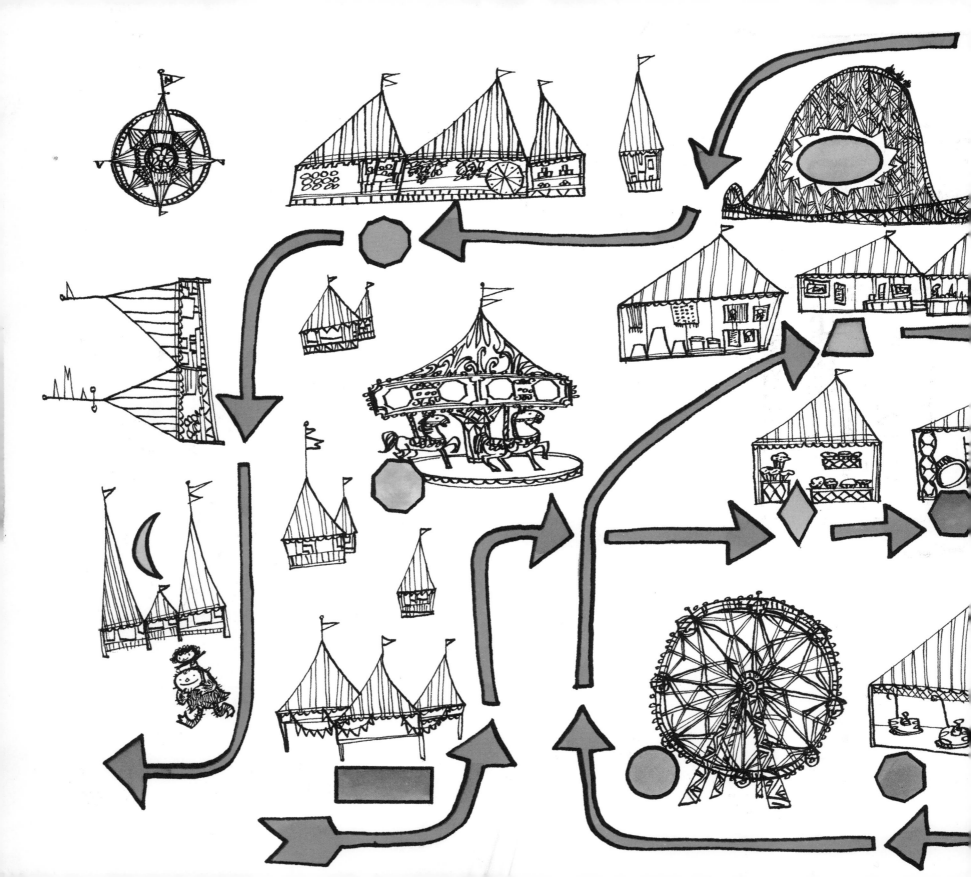